THE STARLIGHT
PRINCESS

AND OTHER PRINCESS STORIES

For Charlie and Mia
B.D.

For my daughters
A.D.

www.dk.com

Produced by **Leapfrog Press Ltd**

Project Editor Naia Bray-Moffatt
Art Editor Sarah Hodder

For Dorling Kindersley
Managing Editor Joanna Devereux
Managing Art Editor Cathy Tincknell
Production Steve Lang

First published in Great Britain in 1999 by
Dorling Kindersley Limited, 9 Henrietta Street, London WC2E 8PS

2 4 6 8 10 9 7 5 3 1

A CIP catalogue record for this book is available from the British Library.

ISBN 0-7513-7432-6

Colour reproduction by Bright Arts in Hong Kong
Printed by Printer Industria Grafica SA

THE STARLIGHT
PRINCESS

AND OTHER PRINCESS STORIES

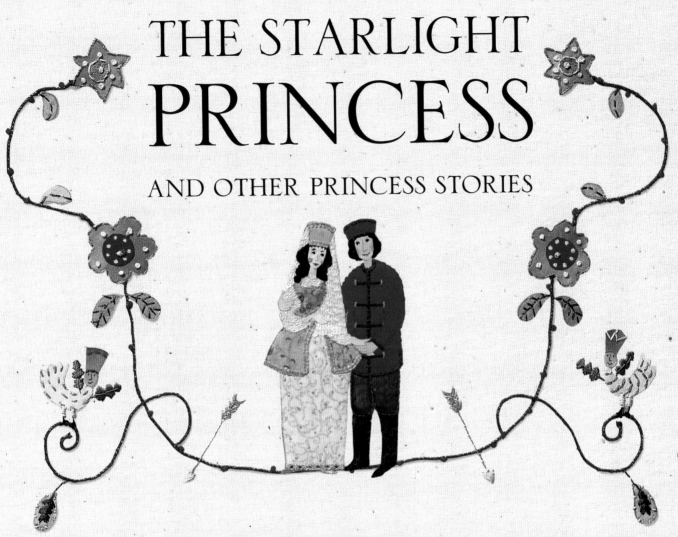

Embroideries by Belinda Downes

Retold by Annie Dalton

www.dk.com

LONDON · NEW YORK · SYDNEY · DELHI

CONTENTS

ARTIST'S INTRODUCTION

I HAVE ALWAYS LOVED HISTORY AND COSTUME DESIGN so I was very excited to be asked to illustrate a collection of princess stories with my embroideries. The opportunity to use rich, luxuriant fabrics and to experiment with different threads and stitches was irresistible.

The stories have been chosen from various countries and cultures around the world. This inspired me to create even more variety by setting each story in a particular historical period. Skipping from age to age between the 14th and the 19th centuries, I studied the costumes and architecture of Medieval Europe, the Mogul period of Northern India, early 19th-century Russia, the tribes of east and southeast Africa and Victorian Britain – all of which gave me a wealth of imagery to work with.

These bookplates show Victorian ladies and an Indian gentleman of the Mogul period.

Once I had decided on a time and a place for the stories, I began to think of different palettes of colour for each one, too. The candlelit, damp interior of the castle in *The Princess & the Pea* needed dark colours. By contrast, the Russian palace of *The Frog Princess* called out for bright reds, yellows and rich shades of inky blue.

My paint palette

After researching the stories, I began by using pen and paper to sketch the characters. I reduced, enlarged and fiddled with expressions, until I was happy with them. Then I traced the drawings onto calico backgrounds, and painted on the faces using fabric paint. For the castles and costumes, I cut out shapes in plain and patterned fabric, and dyed silk for the skies and ground.

I sketch characters in my sketchbooks before starting any embroidery work.

I find it easier to use small hand-held embroidery hoops for detailed work.

In my studio I have baskets full of colourful cottons, muslins, wools, velvets and chiffons. These have been collected over the years – snippets from previous projects and pieces given by friends and family. There are drawers full of everything I might need – from glue and glitter, to beads, buttons, feathers, sequins, braid, lace and gold and silver thread. Even with all this available I somehow still find myself drawn to haberdashery departments and charity shops where I find more exciting bits and pieces to work with. For the Asian tale, *The Starlight Princess*, I visited a number of wonderful sari shops and bought small pieces of cottons and silks in hot pinks, oranges and lime greens.

One of my brimming workbaskets.

When all the pieces of fabric had been cut out and were in place on the background calico, I began adding the extra details. For this book, I chose to decorate mainly by hand and used running and satin stitch over the fabric. When I needed texture I used knots – particularly the bullion knot, a ringletty knot, and the

This piece from The Starlight Princess *uses running stitch and satin stitch.*

French knot. I enjoyed bringing the Welsh terrier dog to life in *King Grizzlebeard* with a profusion of curly French knots. I used the sewing machine only for a scribbly type of stitch called the free-machine stitch. I used it like a pen to outline and fill in. This worked well for the wild hair of the princess when she comes in from the storm in *The Princess & the Pea.*

The Welsh terrier dog in King Grizzlebeard

Working on these stories has been a joy. I've been engrossed and have worked late into the night to finish a piece. I hope my embroideries have enhanced these wonderful stories and will give you as much pleasure to look at as they have given me in creating them.

The storm-blown princess in The Princess & the Pea

Belinda Downes.

11

THE PRINCESS & THE PEA

ONCE THERE WAS A PRINCE who was as handsome as any prince could be. But he was also a pernickety prince – the kind of young man who likes everything just so. And he got it into his head that he could only marry a real princess. He knew perfectly well that a real princess is as rare as a unicorn, but this didn't put him off, not at all.

"I'll just search high and low until I find one," he said cheerfully.

So with two friends for company, off he rode into the wide world to find a real princess to be his bride.

Now, on his travels, as you'd expect, the prince met dozens and dozens of princesses. But whenever he made up his mind to marry one, right at the last minute he'd change his mind again and decide that this princess wasn't a real one after all.

His friends couldn't understand him.

"But the last one was perfect," they cried. "Hair like moonlit silk. Eyes like big blue pansies. What didn't you like? Her dancing?"

"Of course not," sighed the prince. "She's as graceful as a swan."

"Was it her handwriting then? Or her manners?"

"Her handwriting is miles better than mine," said the prince, gloomily. "So are her manners."

"You hate her voice, is that it?"

"How could I?" sighed the prince. "Her voice is as soft as a dove's. Exactly how a princess's voice should be." And he buried his head in his hands.

"Then why won't you marry her?" cried his friends.

"Because I can't be sure she is a real princess," the prince explained.

So the prince and his companions rode sadly home.

"If I can't marry a real princess, then I won't marry at all," he told his mother, the queen.

That night a terrible storm blew up. Lightning crackled across the sky. Thunder boomed. The wind howled and rain battered the windows.

Suddenly, between crashes of thunder, the queen heard a firm tap-tapping at the palace gates, so she threw on her dressing gown and went to see who it could be.

A girl was standing outside. And what a state she was in. The wild weather had tangled her dark curls into a big bush. Rivers of rainwater streamed off her shoulders and splashed off her torn stockings, filling her tough little lace-up boots to overflowing. And every step she took made a sad squelch, like a frog in a ditch. Squish. Squash.

The queen nearly fainted when this sorry-looking creature said that she was a princess who had lost her way in the storm, and asked to stay the night.

"She sounds unusually firm for a princess," thought the queen. "Not a bit like a dove."

The girl wasn't especially graceful either, but marched sturdily across the threshold in her soggy boots – *squish, squash* – and hung her dripping rucksack on the hook in the hall, just as if she lived there!

"Maybe you are a princess and maybe you aren't, young lady," thought the queen. "But you won't fool me for long." And she asked the girl to sign the visitors' book to see if she had the proper handwriting for a princess. But the girl shivered so hard, the ink splurted out of the pen in one big blot.

"Never mind, some soup will warm you up," said the cunning queen. And she heated some cabbage soup left from the servants'

supper and gave it to the girl with a lump of stale bread.

Instead of nibbling daintily like a princess should, the girl sat down at the kitchen table and hungrily spooned up every last drop. She even polished the bowl clean with her crust. When she'd finished, there was a splash of soup on her nose.

"That was the best soup I have ever tasted," she sighed.

"Hmm, maybe it is and maybe it isn't. But we'll settle this business once and for all," muttered the queen. For she knew a thing or two about princesses, if only her clever son had bothered to ask.

So the queen hurried along to the spare bedroom. She whisked all the sheets and blankets off the bed, and off came the mattress too. Then she took a dried pea out of her pocket, placed it in the middle of the bed and put the mattress back on top.

Then on top of the first mattress, the queen piled another mattress, and another, until the bed was twenty mattresses high!

Next she collected up all the spare quilts in the palace;
some with stripes, some with polka dots and some that
badly needed to go to the laundry. But when she
counted them, they came to twenty exactly. The
queen stacked all twenty quilts on top of the
twenty mattresses, until the bed swayed about
like a ship at sea.

At last the girl took off her boots and
clambered sleepily onto this huge, high,
swaying bed, and the queen blew out
the candle – *snuff* – and left her
alone for the night.

Next morning the queen
asked if she had slept well.

But the poor girl was as pale as a ghost.

"Not a wink, I'm afraid," she complained. "Something was sticking into me all night. Look – I'm bruised all over!"

When the queen saw that the girl had felt a tiny pea digging into her through twenty mattresses and twenty quilts, she knew that the girl must be a real princess after all, and ran to tell her son that the search was over.

"Only a real princess has skin so delicate," she told him.

"A real princess at last!" he gasped. "Then if she likes me, we'll marry at once!"

So the prince married the princess and after the wedding was over, the pea was put on show in the Royal Museum,

And if you don't believe me, then go and see it for yourself.

THE FROG PRINCESS

F AR OVER THE SNOWY PLAINS, the frozen rivers and the forests
filled with wolves and magic, there once lived a king who
had three sons. All three were handsome young men, but
the bravest and the best was the youngest, Prince Ivan.

One day the king called his sons to him.

"I'm getting old," he said. "And I want grandchildren before I die."

Then he told each of his sons to take his bow and arrow into the
meadow and shoot an arrow into the air.

"Wherever this arrow lands, you must look for your bride," said the king.

This was a strange way to choose a bride, but no one ever argued with the king in case the world came to an end. So the princes went into the meadow with their bows. The eldest brother turned to the east and shot his arrow. The second brother aimed his arrow to the west. But Prince Ivan drew back his bow with all his strength and shot his arrow straight in front of him. Then they went to see where their arrows had landed.

The eldest brother found his arrow in a courtyard belonging to a noble lord who had a pretty daughter. The second brother had managed to shoot his arrow right through the window of a rich merchant's daughter. But though poor Prince Ivan hunted high and low, he couldn't find his arrow anywhere.

For two days he searched the woods and fields. On the third day his boots began to sink into boggy ground. The prince had wandered into a swamp without noticing. And to his horror, in the middle of this swamp, holding an arrow in her mouth, was a frog.

"Brek-kek-kex," she croaked. "Marry me, Prince Ivan, or you'll never leave this swamp alive."

What could the prince do? He didn't want to marry a frog. But he didn't want to die in a slimy swamp either. Pale with horror, Prince Ivan promised the frog that he would marry her. Then he picked her up and she guided him safely home.

When his brothers saw Prince Ivan coming through the palace gates with his little frog bride, they laughed until their sides hurt and their brides sniggered – *tee hee hee* – behind their hands.

I must be the unhappiest prince who ever lived, thought Prince Ivan. He was just going to beg the frog to release him from his promise, when he noticed the wise expression in her froggy eyes.

"My brothers may laugh if they like," he said to himself. "But I gave my word to marry this frog and if it's my destiny, good shall come of it."

So the king's three sons were married – the eldest to the daughter of a lord, the second to a rich merchant's daughter, and the third, Prince Ivan, to a frog.

After their weddings, the three princes left the palace and found houses of their own. The prince and the frog were surprisingly happy and the prince always treated his bride kindly.

Then one day the king called his sons to him again. And he frowned in that way the sons knew only too well.

"I want to see how neatly these new brides of yours can sew," he said. "Take this linen and ask your wives to make a shirt for me by tomorrow morning."

Since no one argued with the king, for fear of the world ending, the two elder brothers hurried home with the linen. Their wives busily began to cut and stitch. And as they worked they laughed till they cried to think of Prince Ivan's froggy bride trying to sew with her little froggy hands.

When Prince Ivan went home, he didn't breathe a word about his father's test. But the frog saw how unhappy he was, and asked what was wrong.

"He wants you to make a shirt," said the prince. "It isn't fair. You're just a frog."

"Brek-kek-kex," croaked the frog. "Go to bed and rest now, and maybe you'll be wiser tomorrow."

As soon as the prince fell asleep, she asked her servant to cut the linen into small pieces and leave her. Then she took the pieces in her mouth, hopped over to the window, flung them out and croaked, "Winds! Winds! Fly with these pieces and sew me a shirt for the king."

The words were hardly out of her mouth when a shirt, perfectly stitched and finished, came flying back into the room.

When the frog gave him the shirt next day, Prince Ivan couldn't believe it. He put it under his coat and took it to his father's palace. His brothers were there already, dying to show off their wives' needlework.

The eldest brother couldn't wait to show his shirt to the king.

But the king took one glance
before tossing it into the
corner.

"It'll do for one of the
servants I suppose," he said.

Then the king took the
shirt which the merchant's
daughter had stitched.

"Hmmm," he frowned,
"I might wear it to the bath house on a foggy day."

But when he saw the shirt Prince Ivan offered him, the king was
astonished. Not a single seam could be seen in it. And the king
gave orders that this beautiful shirt should only ever be worn on
special feast days.

Ivan's brothers muttered, "She's not a frog, that ugly little wife of
his, she's a witch!"

Well, it wasn't long before the king decided on a second test. So
he called his sons to him. And he drummed his fingers – *rattatattat*
– on his chair, in the way his sons knew only too well.

"Each of your brides must bake me a loaf by tomorrow
morning," he said. "Then we'll see which of my sons has married
the cleverest wife."

Again no one argued with him, in case the world came to an end.

And again when he reached home, Prince Ivan didn't want to tell
the frog what had happened. But she made him tell her.

"It's not fair to ask you to bake bread," said Prince Ivan.
"You're a frog."

"Brek-kek-kex," croaked the frog.
"Go to bed and rest now, and maybe you'll be
wiser tomorrow."

As soon as he fell asleep, the frog
asked her servant to make a paste
of flour and water and to put it in
the cold oven. Then she hopped
to the oven door and said,
"Bread, bread, baker's dough,
bake yourself as white as snow."

The oven door flew open and
there was the loaf cooked to a turn –
white and soft on the inside, and

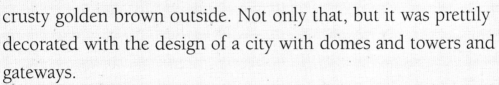

crusty golden brown outside. Not only that, but it was prettily
decorated with the design of a city with domes and towers and
gateways.

Now the other princesses were wildly jealous because the frog's
shirt had been better than theirs. So they sent a little kitchen maid
to spy on the frog to see how she baked her loaf. When the girl
described what she'd seen and heard, they too mixed flour and
water, poured the paste in the cold ovens, and hopefully repeated
the spell.

But the paste just dripped all over the ovens and made a horrible
mess. The angry princesses had to start again and make bread
dough with yeast and hot water, instead of magic. They were in
such bad tempers that one loaf came out burnt, and the other was
still raw.

Next morning, the three sons took their loaves to the king.
The king threw the first one on the floor. "Give it to the beggars at
the gate," he said rudely.

Then he tasted the second loaf. "It might be good enough for my
hounds," he sneered.

Then Prince Ivan unwrapped his bread and the room filled with
magical baking smells. The loaf was as perfect as something from a
fairy tale. It was so delicious that when the king tasted it, he said it
must be kept for a feast.

But before long, the king had a third test for the new brides.

Again he sent for his sons. And he paced up and down the great hall in the way they knew only too well.

"Everyone knows that all princesses must be able to weave in silver and gold," he said. "Take this silk and this gold and silver thread and bring me back three carpets in the morning."

Well no one had ever argued with the king before, and no one argued now. But when Prince Ivan reached home, the frog saw how upset he was and made him tell her about his father's latest test.

"Go to bed and rest now," she croaked. "And maybe you'll be wiser tomorrow."

As soon as he fell asleep, she asked her servant to cut the silk and the silver and gold thread into small pieces. Then, as before, she threw the pieces out of the window.

"Winds! Winds!" she cried. "Fly with these pieces and make me a carpet."

The words were hardly out of her mouth, before the embroidered carpet came flying through the window.

Now once again the jealous princesses had sent the little kitchen maid to spy on the frog. When she described what she'd seen, they were sure the spell would work for them this time. So they cut all their precious materials into pieces, hurled them out of the window and waited.

But no matter how long they waited, no carpets came flying magically through their windows. So the princesses had to send for more materials, and they sat up all night long, weaving angrily.

When the king saw the carpets the angry princesses had made, he shook his head.

"Put this one in the stable," he said to his eldest son. "It might do as a horse blanket." And to his second son he said, "I suppose the servants could wipe their feet on it."

Then Prince Ivan unrolled his carpet, and the king was so astonished he couldn't think of a thing to say. It was the most beautiful pattern anyone had ever seen. At last, the king said that this carpet should be put in his treasury and brought out only on special feast days.

"Now, my dear children," said the king, all smiles for once. "Since your wives have done everything I asked, bring them here tomorrow night, and we'll eat, drink, dance and be merry."

The two older brothers grinned.

"Ivan's frog wife may know a few magic tricks," they whispered.

"But when it comes down to it, she's just a frog. Everyone will laugh till their buttons fly off when they see her."

Prince Ivan went home in despair.

"You sewed the shirt and baked the bread and you wove the carpet," he said to his frog bride. "And I'm grateful. But in the end you're a frog and my brothers' wives are beautiful women. How can I take you to the feast?"

"Brek-kek-kex," croaked the frog. "Go to bed and rest now, and maybe you'll be wiser tomorrow."

Next day the frog said mysteriously, "You must trust me, my dear. Go to the palace and I'll follow later. When you hear horses' hooves, say, 'Here comes my poor little frog in her box'. And you will see what you will see."

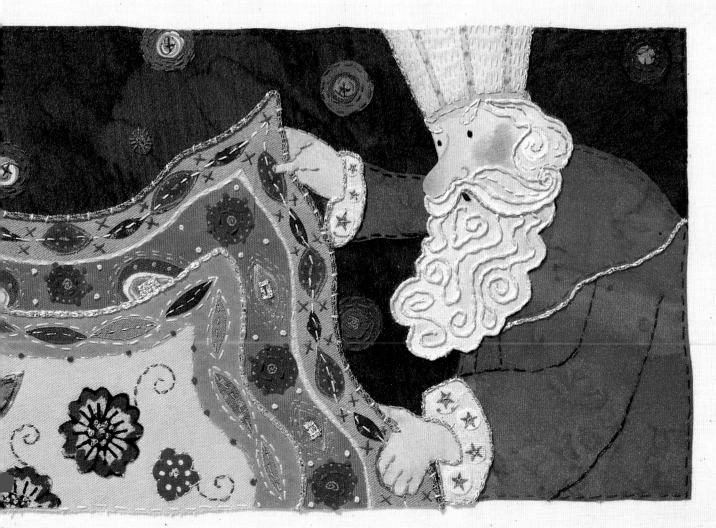

At her words, Prince Ivan's heart felt wonderfully light and his worries fell away. For strange as it may seem, he had come to love the frog.

"Neither my father nor my brothers were ever as kind as you, my little frog bride," he said softly. "Why should I care what they think of me?" And he set off for the palace.

As soon as the prince was out of sight, the frog hopped to the window and called, "Winds! Winds! Bring me a carriage with six white horses!"

Six white horses trotted up, drawing a golden coach behind them. With a little shiver of magic, the frog threw off her skin. And in her place stood a princess so dazzlingly lovely that for a moment the moon hid herself behind a cloud.

Meanwhile the guests were arriving at the palace. When Ivan's older brothers saw Ivan by himself, they sneered, "Why didn't you bring your lovely bride? Haven't you got an old dishcloth to dress her in?"

But Prince Ivan ignored them. Just then everyone heard the sound of trotting hooves and rumbling wheels.

"Don't worry about that," he said quickly. "It's only my poor little frog in a box."

The whole court rushed outside to see this strange sight. But a golden coach drew up, pulled by six milk-white horses. The beautiful princess stepped out and smiled at her astonished husband. "My name is Vassilissa the Wise," she said. "A wicked magician turned me into a frog, but your love for me broke the spell."

Then they danced past the prince's brothers and their jealous brides. They danced past the king, who was already frowning slightly, as if he might be thinking up some new test.

The couple went on dancing right out of the palace door and into the starry winter's night. Where they danced to no one knows. But you can be sure that the prince and his wise princess lived happily ever after.

KING GRIZZLEBEARD

THERE WAS ONCE A PRINCESS so beautiful that any prince who saw her portrait instantly became desperate to marry her. Unfortunately, as soon as they actually met her these princes quickly changed their minds. For the princess had got in the habit of poking fun at every suitor who came near her.

Now she truly didn't mean to be spiteful, but she had an extremely lively mind. And since no one had ever taught her anything useful, the princess had nothing to do with her days except wait for the latest adoring young man to turn up at the palace and decide if she fancied him or not.

And every time she found herself face to
face with some earnest new prince or duke, a terrible
rudeness came over her and shocking remarks tumbled out of her
mouth like toads.

Well, the king was running out of patience, for his daughter
wouldn't be young for ever. So he held a great feast and invited all
her latest admirers at once, to get it over with. Then he seated these
eager kings, princes, dukes and earls in rows of splendid golden
chairs.

"All you've got to do, young lady, is walk up and down in your
new dress and choose which young man you want to marry," the
king told her. "Couldn't be simpler."

But the moment the princess walked into the hall, she could feel
her mind begin to fill with witty, but unkind, comments.

Before she could stop herself, the princess was making her terrible jokes again.

The first prince she passed was small and rather plump.

"I wouldn't have that little tub of lard if you paid me," she giggled naughtily.

The second was extremely tall.

"'Is that a prince or did all the ribbons blow off the maypole?" she inquired.

And so it went on.

But when she came to one extremely handsome king with curly strands of silver in his beard, the princess laughed until tears rolled down her cheeks.

"I've got the perfect name for this one, everyone," she cried. "From now on you've all got to call him King Grizzlebeard."

Her father was so ashamed of his daughter's outrageous behaviour that he vowed he'd hand her over to the first man who came to the palace, even if he turned out to be a beggar.

The very next day a musician began to sing under the windows.

"Bring him in," said the king when he heard him.

The servants brought in a ragged young man. When he had sung for everyone, the king said, "You sang so well, I'd like to give you my daughter for your wife."

Of course the princess wept and pleaded but the king's mind was made up.

So the princess was married to the musician.

When the ceremony was over, the king said,"Now you must go out into the world with your husband."

The musician and the princess left the palace and set out walking. After some distance, they came to a sweet-smelling forest.

"Who does this wonderful forest belong to?" asked the princess.

"To King Grizzlebeard," said the musician. "It would have been yours if you'd married him."

"Oh dear, lovely King Grizzlebeard, how I wish I'd married you," thought the unhappy princess.

A little later, the couple came to fine meadows where beautiful horses grazed in the sun.

"Who owns all this?" asked the princess.

"King Grizzlebeard, of course," said the musician. "They would have been yours, too, if you'd married him."

"Oh dear, lovely King Grizzlebeard, how I wish I'd married you," thought the princess longingly.

Not long after that, they saw a great city in the distance.

"And I suppose King Grizzlebeard owns that city, as well," she joked.

"Naturally," said the musician in surprise. "It would have been yours if you'd married him."

And when she heard this, the princess burst out crying.

Just then they reached a poky little cottage.

"What a sty, what a hole in the ground," cried the princess in horror. "Who could possibly live here?"

"Why, this is your new home, my love," said the musician. "Where you and I will live together to the end of our days."

"But where are our servants?" she cried.

"We don't need servants. You're here now, to do anything that needs to be done," said her husband cheerfully, "and you can begin by cooking supper."

Of course the princess had never even learnt how to boil an egg, so the musician had to help her. Even so, it wasn't much of a meal. And then they went to bed.

So it went on, until after two days there was no food left in the larder.

"We can't go on like this, spending our money and earning nothing. I'll teach you to make baskets if you like. Then we can sell them," said the musician.

He went into the water meadows and cut willow branches for the princess to weave. But though she tried as hard as she could, her fingers quickly became very sore.

"I can see this isn't the work for you," said the musician. "Maybe you'll do better at spinning."

So she sat down at the spinning wheel and tried as hard as she could, but the threads cut her tender fingers till the blood ran.

"No wonder your father wanted to give you away," sighed the musician. "You can't do anything useful. Never mind, I'll get a stall in the market and you can sell pots and pans."

"Don't do that," begged the princess. "If someone from my father's court sees me, I'll die of shame."

"And if you don't work, you'll die of hunger," said the musician. "Which is it to be?"

As it turned out, the princess did surprisingly well at selling pots and pans. She was so pleased with herself, she hummed all the way home.

A few days later, when the couple had spent all her earnings, her husband brought more pots for her to sell. But as soon as the princess set out her pots in the corner of the market, a drunken soldier rode his horse against her stall, smashing her goods to pieces.

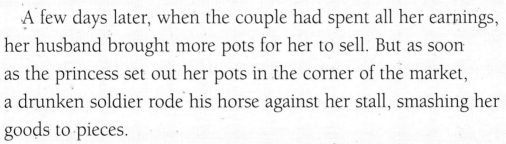

The princess ran home sobbing and told her husband what had happened.

"Never mind," he said. "They're always looking for kitchen maids in King Grizzlebeard's palace. And you can bring us home any food which is left over."

So now from morning to night, the princess worked as a kitchen maid, helping the cook sweep and scrub and peel and chop.

One day, the cook called her to look out of the window to watch the king passing by, on his way to be married.

The princess gazed at the great procession of lords and ladies in their fine clothes. A tear slid down her face to think of the life she might have had, if only she had been wiser. Then the cook filled the princess's basket with delicious left-overs, as usual, and she set off home.

Just as she was leaving the palace, in strode the king in his magnificent, golden, wedding clothes. "Won't you come and dance with me?" he asked her.

When the princess recognised King Grizzlebeard's handsome face, she began to tremble and wished herself dead and buried. I don't blame him for making fun of me, she thought. After the way I treated him.

Without a word she allowed the king to take her hand and lead her into the hall. But he whirled her so wildly round the dance floor that little left-over pastries flew out of her basket, right in front of everyone.

The princess fled from the hall, weeping with shame, but the king caught up with her on the palace steps.

"Don't you recognise me?" he said gently. "I'm the musician who brought you to my tiny cottage and made you weave and spin.

"I'm also the soldier who tipped over your stall. I didn't do these things to punish you, but because I love you with all my heart. Now you know more of the world than you did before, it's time to hold our marriage feast. That's if you'll still have me," he added.

Of course, now the princess knew what a good man the king was. So she quickly washed her face and put on her wedding robes and the guests feasted and danced and sang for a week or more.

Then the witty princess and her wise King Grizzlebeard lived happily ever after.

THE STARLIGHT PRINCESS

ONCE UPON A TIME, a king and queen had a baby daughter. The king was so proud of her, that by the time he finished praising her silky hair, her golden brown skin and her pearly little toe-nails, the baby princess was already three days old.

Then a soft breeze began to blow, carrying the night scent of jasmine and the lullabies of frogs and crickets into the room.

The king looked up from the cradle in surprise and realised that darkness was falling outside the nursery. Yet indoors it was still as bright as day.

"Why is it so light in here?" he asked his wife. "I didn't light the lamps. Did you?"

"I wondered when you'd notice," said the queen, dreamily. "It's our little girl. I think she gets it from my side of the family."

And for the first time the king noticed that the baby princess was shining like a star. A dazzling silvery light poured from her, filling the nursery and turning night into day.

Our daughter is clearly a very unusual child. I must take great care of her, thought the king.

For the first few years of his daughter's life, the king refused to let her leave the palace in case something happened to her.

But as she grew older, the princess had ideas of her own.

"I don't want to upset you, but my light is meant to be shared with everyone," she said firmly to her parents on her seventh birthday.

After that, each evening at dusk, the little princess climbed onto the palace roof. There she sat until midnight, lighting up the kingdom with her silvery rays.

Now in a neighbouring country, a wealthy Rajah and his wife also wanted a child. And when their son was born, he had a special gift, too. Before he could even speak, this tiny boy understood the language of every wild creature who shares this earth with us.

"I don't know how such a peculiar talent will be of use to him in his life," said the Rajah. "But I'm still very proud of him."

Then one day the Rajah's wife heard about the princess who lit up her father's kingdom with her magical starlight.

"If our son finds out about her, he'll run off and marry her one day, I know he will," she said despairingly.

"Don't worry, my love. He'll never know of her existence," the Rajah promised.

The years passed and the Rajah's son grew to be a brave, handsome young man. But although he was allowed to roam freely on three sides of his father's land, his mother made him promise on her life that he would never venture into the fourth side. She was convinced that if her son ever heard of the princess, he would want her for his bride.

Then one day, while he was out hunting, the Rajah's son stopped to rest in the shade of a mango tree. A flock of parrots settled in the branches and began chattering amongst themselves. The young man listened with growing wonder to their description of a princess so magical that her beauty turned night into day.

"I must travel the world till I find her or I won't know another minute's happiness," he cried. He hurried home to tell his parents.

With tears pouring down her face, his mother begged him not to go. But when she saw his mind was made up, she gave him a packet of sweetmeats made with her own hands, and wished him a safe journey.

The young Rajah rode for hours. At last he was so hot and dusty, he stopped to bathe in a stream. But when he unwrapped the sweets his mother had given him, each one had a tiny ant inside it.

"Well, since you gentlemen got here first, you may eat them all," he said.

At that, the king ant waved his feelers gratefully in the air.

"When you need us, just think of us and we will help you in return," said the ant.

The Rajah's son thanked the ants in their own language and continued on his way.

After he had ridden for an hour or more, he heard a beast roaring with pain. The Rajah sprang down from his horse and searched the undergrowth, until he found a tiger who had got a thorn stuck in his paw.

"May I help?" asked the Rajah's son in tiger language. The tiger allowed him to examine his injured paw and, very gently, the Rajah removed the thorn.

The tiger and his mate rubbed their heads against him to show their gratitude and said, "When you need us, just think of us and we'll help you in return."

He thanked them and went on his way, riding deep into the jungle. Suddenly, in a clearing he came upon three holy men. They were arguing fiercely, pushing and poking each other like boys. When they saw the Rajah's son, the three men called him over, begging him to settle their quarrel. They explained that they had a magic carpet that would take a man anywhere he wanted to go. But they couldn't agree which of them it belonged to.

The Rajah's son decided to trick them and get this wonderful carpet for himself.

"That is easily solved," he said aloud. "I'll fire an arrow into the jungle. Whoever finds the arrow first, shall keep the carpet."

"This young Rajah is almost as wise as we are," said the first holy man, amazed.

The Rajah's son hid his smiles and fired his arrow into the jungle as far as he could. The moment the three men dashed into the trees, he unrolled the carpet and jumped onto it, crying, "Take me to the beautiful princess who turns night into day."

The magic carpet sailed up into the evening sky. It skimmed over the tops of trees, over temples, towers and wonderful gardens, until at last the young Rajah saw a silvery light streaming towards him. When he saw it, he knew he had found his beloved at last.

The young Rajah didn't want to land on her roof unannounced, like a robber. So he commanded the carpet to take him to the princess's bedroom where he secretly left a beautiful rose on her pillow. Then the carpet spirited him away again.

The following evening, he commanded the carpet to take him to the princess's room again, and he left a second rose on her pillow.

But on the third night, instead of roses, the Rajah's son himself was waiting for the princess when she climbed down from the roof.

He took a gold ring from his finger, saying, "If your father will allow it, I would be honoured to marry you."

The princess knew at once that this was the husband she had waited for all her life. So they went straight to the king and asked for his blessing. But the king said he wasn't going to let his beautiful daughter marry the first good-looking rascal who sailed through her window on a magic carpet.

"I'll give you three tasks," thundered the king. "If you succeed, my daughter shall be yours. If you fail, I'll have you put to death."

Next day at sunrise, the king took the Rajah's son into a courtyard, showing him a heap of mustard seeds as high as an elephant and many jars.

"Crush these seeds and squeeze out every drop of oil," said the king. "I'll return at sunset. And if you've failed to complete the task, you will lose your life."

When the king left, the Rajah's son put his head in his hands.

"I need help," he said aloud. "But who could help with such an impossible task?"

"I can," said a tiny voice.

The Rajah's son looked down at his feet in surprise and there was the king ant waving his feelers at him. Behind him a long column of ants marched steadily into the courtyard.

"Lie down and sleep. My troops will do what needs to be done," said the king ant.

So the Rajah's son lay down and slept. When he woke again, the ants had crushed every last mustard seed, filling every jar

to the brim with golden oil. But when the king came at sunset and saw the brimming jars, he only said, "My daughter is not yet yours. There are two tasks left to do."

Next day, the king took the Rajah's son to a distant part of the palace and unlocked an ancient door. On the other side was a dirty, dismal room with crumbling walls and broken windows.

"This room is haunted by evil demons. Even wild birds are afraid to come here. Kill the demons by sunset, or it will be the worse for you."

With these words the king pushed the Rajah's son into the haunted room and locked the door.

How could one person, even if he was the brave son of a Rajah, defeat demons from the other world? The Rajah's son had no idea.

"I need help," he said. "But who could help with such an impossible task?"

"We can," roared a voice, and two tigers sprang into the room.

"I think you'd better shut your eyes," said the male tiger. "My beautiful wife and I will do everything that needs to be done."

Just then, with shrieks of glee, the demons burst out of their hiding places. But before they could attack the Rajah with their fiendish teeth and claws, the tigers knocked them down, baring *their* teeth and claws and roaring ferociously.

The young Rajah quickly closed his eyes, so he never saw exactly what the tigers were doing. It made a terrible noise and went on for hours. But when he dared to open his eyes again, both demons and tigers had vanished. Then a tiny bird fluttered onto the windowsill and began to sing its sweet evening song, so he knew that the demons had gone for ever.

When the king unlocked the room at sunset, he seemed surprised to find the Rajah's son alive. But all he said was, "My daughter isn't yours yet. There is one task left."

On the final day the king took the Rajah's son into the jungle.

"Do you see that tall tree?" he growled. "Split it in half by sunset or you'll lose your life, this time for sure."

The king handed him a hatchet and strode away.

Well, that's not so difficult, thought the Rajah's son. Then he ran his finger along the hatchet blade, and found to his horror that it was made of candle wax.

The Rajah's son was in despair. "Who is left to help me with such an impossible task?" he cried.

"I am," said a voice.

The princess herself appeared beside him. Before he could explain, she quickly pulled a silky hair from her head. Then she laid the hair carefully along the wax blade of the hatchet.

"Now ask the tree to split itself in half for me," she said.

The young Rajah did as she told him. With a tremendous cracking sound the tree split itself joyfully in two.

"Now you're mine!" he cried.

"And you're mine, don't forget," the princess pointed out.

So the Rajah's son and the princess were married and all the wild creatures celebrated. Afterwards they flew back to the Rajah's house on the magic carpet.

At first the king and queen missed the starlight princess terribly. But one evening the queen had the bright idea of climbing onto the palace roof, so they could see the silvery light streaming towards them through the dusk.

THE SLEEPING BEAUTY

ONCE THERE WAS A KING AND QUEEN who had everything
that a king and queen could possibly want. Their castle
had so many wonderful rooms they never had time to
count them. Their garden was planted with the loveliest roses ever
seen in this world. They had a stable full of horses, hives full of
honey and a kitchen with a cook, a butler and dozens of cheerful
little maids to sweep and polish and curtsey.

But even though they had all this and more besides, the young
queen cried herself to sleep every night. For the only thing she
wanted was the one thing she didn't have. A beautiful baby of
her own.

But for all her wishing and weeping, no baby came.

Then one night she went sorrowfully into the garden in her nightdress and sat beside the fountain. All at once, a tiny fish popped its head out of the water.

"Don't be sad," it said. "You'll have a baby daughter before the year is over." Then the fish vanished back into the water.

Sure enough, the fish's words came true and before the year was over the queen gave birth to a beautiful baby girl.

The king was so delighted, he decided to hold a feast to celebrate.

"Don't forget to ask the fairies," the queen reminded him. "They always give such unusual presents."

Now, there were thirteen fairies in this kingdom but it just so happened that one of them really gave the king the horrors. She kept sneezing all the time for one thing. And she always wore the same old coat, which smelt of mice. The thought of her coming anywhere near his sweet little baby made the king break out in goosepimples.

"I, er, seem to remember we've only got twelve gold dishes," said the king quickly. "I'll just ask the butler to check."

To the butler's surprise, there were only twelve dishes in the cupboard. (There had been thirteen the last time he looked.)

So when the invitations were sent out, only twelve fairies were invited; the ones who didn't smell of mice.

On the day of the feast, everyone crowded into the banqueting hall with gifts for the baby princess. Then the fairies gathered around the cradle. One after another they waved their wands and in sweet voices sang out blessings for the baby's happiness:

"Beauty," said one.

"Delight," said the second.

"Wisdom," said the third.

And so it went on.

Just as the twelfth fairy was going to speak, the door suddenly burst open and in strode the thirteenth fairy sneezing furiously.

The king turned pale. "Oh dear," he whispered.

The fairy elbowed her way to the front, until she stood breathing heavily over the cradle. Then she pulled a filthy old handkerchief out of her sleeve and waved it in the baby princess's face.

"You can forget everything they just said, ducky," she screeched. "Because when you're fifteen you'll prick your finger on a spindle and fall down dead. And if you don't like it, you can blame your father. Twelve gold plates - bah -ah -ah -tishoo!"

Then she vanished in mid-sneeze, leaving a terrible smell of mice behind her.

The baby began to wail with terror. The king clenched his fists, for this terrible calamity was all his fault. The queen burst into tears.

Then everyone realised that the twelfth fairy was speaking.

"Sssh," the guests told each other.

After all the shouting, the fairy's voice sounded as peaceful as falling snow.

"Don't be afraid," she said. "I haven't made my wish yet. And though I can't use it to undo our sister's curse, I can soften the harm she's done. I promise this little princess won't die. Instead she will only fall asleep for a hundred years."

Well, of course the king and queen thanked the fairy politely. But after everyone had gone home, the king paced up and down, bellowing that he wasn't having any kind of curse put on his child, whether it was his fault or not.

"I'll buy up every single spindle in my kingdom and personally see they're all destroyed!"

And that's what he did. "Now we can forget the whole thing," he told the queen.

The years flew past and one by one all the good fairies' wishes for the young princess came true. As she grew, she became beautiful, wise and a delight to everyone who knew her. Soon no one even remembered the thirteenth fairy's curse.

When the princess turned fifteen her parents held a birthday party for her. There were jugglers and fire-eaters, acrobats and

conjurers. The king's cook baked a special birthday cake in the shape of a swan and when the princess blew out her candles, everyone shouted, "Make a wish!"

"I've already got everything I want," said the princess. Then she laughed. "But I need to run around a bit before I've got room for any cake. Let's play hide and seek. You hide and I'll come after you."

The princess counted to one hundred and went hunting around the castle. But the girls had hidden in such obvious places she found them easily. All except for one.

The princess searched everywhere she could think of, but she still couldn't find her friend. "I give up," she called at last.

Then all at once she found herself at the bottom of a narrow stairway leading to an old, forgotten tower. She was just wondering why she'd never noticed this part of the castle before, when floating down from the tower she heard the sweetest humming sound. Somehow this magical sound drove everything else out of her head, and forgetting her friend, she began to climb the stairs. The higher she climbed the sweeter the humming seemed to grow, until at last she stood outside a door. A shining key stood in the lock. She turned it and the door flew open. Inside a little room sat an old lady, spinning busily.

"What are you doing?" asked the princess.

"Why, I'm just spinning, ducky," said the old lady. There was such a strong smell of mice in the room, the princess had to hold her breath. But for some reason she found herself taking a step nearer. And another. She couldn't help it, for the wicked enchantment was already working.

"What's that bright little thing dancing this way and that?" the princess said, dreamily. "May I try?" she asked, stretching out her hand to take it. At that moment the spindle pricked her and she fell to the floor as though she was dead.

But the princess was not dead, only in an enchanted sleep. And as she slept a gentle breeze began to stir. It riffled and ruffled the roses in the garden until all the petals came loose and great drifts of them blew into every part of the castle.

Wherever the petals blew, everyone fell into a deep sleep: the king and queen and all their court, the horses in the stables, the dogs in the yard, the pigeons on the rooftops and the flies on the walls. The soldiers on the battlements slumped to the ground. The fire in the hearth stopped blazing. The roasting meat stood still on the spit. The cook who had just raised her hand to box the ears of the cheeky kitchen boy abruptly let him go, and they both fell fast asleep. And with a curious whirring sound, the castle clock stopped ticking. Inside the castle gates, time itself stood still.

Soon a hedge of wild briars grew up around the castle.

With every year the hedge grew taller and thicker, until at last the whole castle was hidden behind a great forest of brambles, and not even the rooftops could be seen.

As summers came and went, tales of an enchanted princess spread to far distant kingdoms. From time to time, several king's sons tried to fight their way through the forest of briars to find her. But the thorns slashed their clothes to ribbons, clutching at the princes like witches' fingers, so that some young men stuck fast in the thicket and died.

After many years, a prince travelled through this kingdom. And one day he met an old man who told him about the rose thicket and the enchanted castle in which a lovely princess slept with all her court.

As soon as he heard this story, the prince was suddenly sure he already knew this princess, and had walked and talked with her in his dreams. "I'll find her and see if I can break this terrible spell," he said at once.

"Many bold young princes have tried and failed," said the old man. "Some even lost their lives."

"Oh, I don't scare that easily," laughed the prince.

However, when he saw the thicket, his heart nearly failed him. Dozens of hats and swords belonging to previous princes were tangled up in the briars.

But that day the hundred years finally came to an end. Before the prince could draw his own weapon to hack down the brambles, the thicket magically burst into flower.

The briars fell back harmlessly to let him through. Yet once he passed, they closed silently behind him again.

At last the prince reached the enchanted castle. The dogs were fast asleep in the courtyard. The horses slept in the stables. The pigeons had their heads under their wings. In the kitchen, the cook stood as still as a statue, raising her hand to box the kitchen boy's ears as she had done for a hundred years.

The castle was so still, there was no sound anywhere, except the faint creak of the prince's boots as he wandered from room to room searching for the princess.

When he found the narrow stairway, he knew at once that this was the place. As he began to climb, the castle grew so still, it seemed to be holding its breath.

At the top of the tower the prince found a door opening into a chamber. There inside was the beautiful princess of his dreams, lying deep in an enchanted sleep.

Before he had time to think, he bent down and kissed her. And something astonishing happened. The moment she felt his kiss, the princess stretched and murmured. Then she opened her eyes, looking wonderingly around her.

When she saw the prince she was not in the least afraid, but smiled as if she'd known him all her life.

"You were in my dreams," she said.

"And you were in mine," the prince told her.

They left the chamber where she had slept for so long and as they ran downstairs, they heard a loud whirring sound from the castle clock as time started again and the castle slowly began to come back to life.

The king and queen and all their court opened their eyes and gazed around in surprise. The horses stamped and peered over their stable doors whinnying, wanting to be fed. The pigeons flew away into the fields. The fire in the hearth blazed once more. The cook scratched her head, wondering why she'd been so cross with the kitchen boy. And while she was thinking, he dodged under her arm and raced out of the kitchen laughing at her.

So the princess and the prince were married and went to live in a castle of their own.

And everyone lived happily ever after.

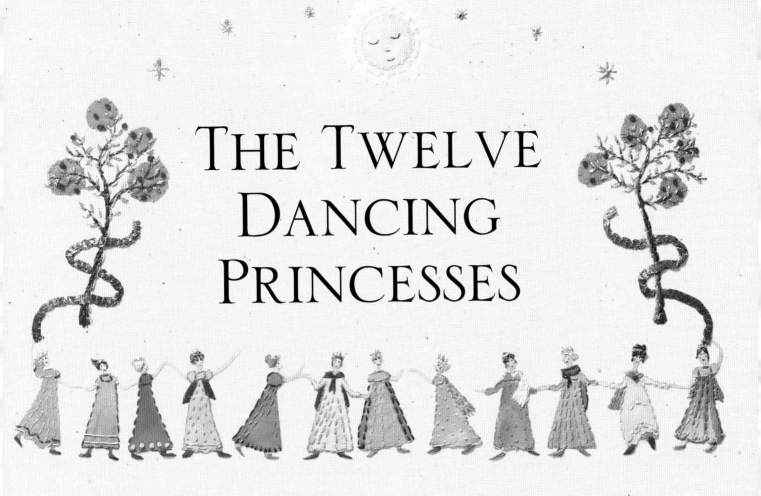

THE TWELVE DANCING PRINCESSES

ONCE UPON A TIME, a king had twelve daughters. These girls were up to mischief all day long as you'd expect. But each evening at sunset they lay down, good as gold, in their twelve narrow beds. The king kissed the princesses on their smooth, pretty foreheads and locked their bedroom door to keep them safe while they slept.

But something strange was going on in that palace. Every morning, the princesses' shoes were worn into holes, just as if they had been dancing all night.

How was this possible? Where did the princesses go while the rest of the world was sleeping? Everyone wondered but nobody knew. The princesses themselves just smiled faraway smiles, as if they didn't know what the fuss was about.

It was such a worry to the king that he issued a proclamation saying that whoever solved the mystery could choose the princess he liked best to be his bride.

The very next day, up rode a young prince determined to solve the mystery once and for all and win himself a princess at the same time.

The king entertained him royally until nightfall. Then he showed the prince to the bed-chamber right next to the one where the twelve princesses lay, good as gold, in their twelve narrow beds.

All the prince had to do, said the king, was leave his door open a crack and watch where his daughters went at night, then report to the king in the morning.

"Is that all?" thought the prince. "First I'll have a little snooze, then I'll begin."

But when he woke, to his horror the sun was already high in the sky, and the princesses had been up to their tricks again, for their slippers were worn into shreds.

On the second and third night, the prince did no better, so the king had him thrown into the darkest dungeon. Several other princes turned up to try their luck after this, but they ended up in the dungeon, too.

One day a soldier was passing through the kingdom. He'd been wounded in battle. He was just wondering what to do with the rest of his life now that soldiering was out of the question, when an old woman stepped out from among the trees and asked him where he was going.

"I hardly know where I'm going, or what to do next," said the soldier. "I suppose I could always find out where those princesses go to dance," he joked. "Then in time I might become king."

"Is it a king you want to be?" said the old woman. "That's easy enough. Just take care not to drink the wine one of the princesses brings you, and when she leaves, pretend to be fast asleep."

Then the old woman gave the soldier a cloak. "The moment you put this on you'll become invisible," she said. "You can follow the princesses wherever they go and they'll never guess you're there."

This was too good a chance to miss. So the soldier went to the king and offered his services there and then. The king welcomed him as politely as he had welcomed the others, and ordered him a set of fine new clothes. When evening came, the soldier was led to his bed-chamber. He'd hardly been there a minute, when in came the eldest princess, with a glass of wine for him.

The soldier was careful not to drink a drop out of it, and as soon as she left he poured the wine out of the window. Then he lay down and started to snore as if he was sound asleep.

When the twelve princesses heard him, they stuffed their fingers into their mouths, trying not to laugh. "If he wants to end up in the dungeon like those other fools, good luck to him," said the eldest.

Then the princesses jumped out of bed and pulled open all the drawers and cupboards. Like lightning, those girls whisked out their dancing dresses and their finest jewels and put them on. Quickly, quickly they fastened buttons and brushed each other's long hair. And all the time they whispered and giggled and pulled silly faces in the mirror, for all the world like girls getting ready for a ball.

Finally, they put on the twelve pairs of new silk slippers that had arrived that very day from the royal shoe-maker and skipped about as if they couldn't wait to start dancing.

All except the youngest princess, who looked pale. "Something's wrong. I can feel it," she said.

"You silly goose," said her eldest sister. "Have you forgotten what happened to those other fine heroes who promised to watch us? That solider had one eye half-shut before I left him. Even without our sleeping potion he'd be snoring like a pig. But if it will put your mind at rest, see for yourself!" she said.

All the princesses peeped in at the soldier. He snored louder than ever.

"Told you so," said the eldest princess. And she went straight to her own bed and clapped her hands briskly. The bed sank down through the floor and a little trap door flew open.

One by one, the princesses vanished through the door. But the soldier was spying on them and saw everything that they did. He quickly threw on the cloak the old woman had given him and hurried after them.

Half-way down the stairs the soldier accidentally trod on the back of the youngest princess's dress.

"Someone's following us!" she cried in alarm. "He grabbed me in the dark!"

"You silly pudding," said the eldest princess. "That was just a nail in the wall."

Down the winding stairs flew the twelve princesses, with the invisible soldier close behind them, until at last they reached a door.

On the other side of it was a grove of trees with glittering silver leaves. The soldier broke off a twig as he passed by. *Cra-ack*, it went!

The youngest princess turned paler than ever. "Did you hear that?" she cried.

"You little noodle," said her eldest sister. "Don't you know that is our princes shouting with joy because we're on our way!"

The princesses hurried on, with the soldier close behind them.

Next they reached a second grove of shining trees, and the leaves were made out of purest gold. Soon afterwards they came to the most dazzling grove of all, where the leaves were all diamonds.

The soldier broke off two twigs. *Cra-ack! Cra-ack!*

The youngest princess cried out with fear at the sounds. But her sister insisted it was only their princes shouting.

On they went until they came to a lake, where there were twelve boats with twelve handsome princes in them, waiting.

Each princess stepped into a boat. This was a problem for the soldier for the boats were small.

"They say three's a crowd," he muttered. "But we'll have to make the best of it." And he jumped into the same boat as the youngest princess.

As they rowed over the lake, the prince mopped his brow and said, "This boat seems so heavy today."

"It's probably the heat," said the princess. "I'm rather warm myself."

The princes rowed right up to a great castle. Light streamed from all its windows and suddenly the air filled with music so lively that the soldier's toes began tapping this way and that. The princes and princesses hurried into the castle and began to dance the night away, every prince with his own princess.

The soldier danced invisibly with each couple in turn. But when any of the princesses was given a goblet of wine, he swigged it down quickly before she managed to put it to her lips.

The youngest princess was terribly scared when she noticed this, but whenever she tried to mention it, her big sister hushed her.

The princesses danced until three in the morning. By then their shoes were worn to ribbons, so they had to stop whether they liked it or not.

The princes rowed the princesses back over the lake. This time, the soldier shared the boat with the eldest princess, and her prince grumbled about the unusually heavy boat.

When they reached the shore, the princes and princesses called their goodbyes to each other, and promised to meet the next night.

The soldier ran on ahead and dived into bed, boots and all.

The princesses were completely out of breath by the time they had climbed the secret stairs. But when they heard the soldier snoring in the next room they giggled and said, "You see – we were perfectly safe the whole time."

Then yawning and rubbing their eyes, the tired princesses pulled off their dresses, bundled their clothes out of sight, kicked off their shoes and fell asleep the minute their heads touched the pillows.

The soldier grinned to himself in the dark and decided not to mention his adventures to the king just yet. He hadn't had so much fun for years.

So on the second and third nights he followed the princesses again and everything happened as before. The princesses danced until their shoes fell to pieces and then went sleepily home to bed.

But on the third night, the soldier hid one of the golden goblets inside his cloak.

Next morning the soldier was called before the king. The twelve princesses hid behind the door, giggling, dying to see the soldier marched off to join the others in the dungeons.

"So tell me," demanded the king. "Did you find out where my twelve princesses dance at night?"

"I certainly did, your majesty," said the soldier, cheerfully. "With twelve princes in a castle under the ground." Then he produced the three twigs he had broken from the magic groves, and the golden cup he had stolen from the castle.

When the king saw these things, he called his daughters and asked if the soldier was telling the truth.

The princesses realised that it was no use trying any more of their tricks, and confessed that every word was true.

"Which of my daughters would you like to marry?" sighed the king.

"I'm not so young as I was, so I'll take the eldest if that's all right with you, your majesty," the soldier replied.

So the soldier and his princess were married that very day.

And when the old king died, some years later, the soldier became king in his place. And a very good king he made, too.

THE EGG PRINCE

L ONG AGO IN AFRICA there was a great king who loved his queen. But one day she caught a fever and it was obvious that she was going to die.

The king went into her hut to say goodbye.

"Husband," said his wife, "I have given you many daughters. But now I can never give you a son. So I have one last gift for you. Bring me whatever you find in the corner of the hut."

Feeling foolish, her husband did as she asked. Behind a roll of mats he found the most monstrous egg he'd ever seen.

81

"Care for it as if it were your son," said his wife in a weak voice. "And see what happens."

The king just thought she was feverish and talking nonsense. Yet when his queen died he couldn't bring himself to throw her strange gift away. He wrapped the egg lovingly in a beautiful cloth and put it in a safe place.

Weeks and months went past. But the king kept remembering his wife's dying words and the son she had longed to give him.

One day he was invited to a feast in a nearby village. Everyone danced and sang late into the night. Everyone except the king, who missed his queen too much to dance or sing. Then he noticed a fawn-like girl amongst the dancers. She danced with such fire and grace that he asked who she was.

"That's Lebou, our king's daughter," he was told. "She's as strong as she is beautiful. She can run faster than our finest warriors."

That night the king tossed and turned in his bed. If my wife had borne a son, Princess Lebou would have been his bride, he thought. At last the king fell asleep and dreamt that he had a son. But the prince seemed unhappy.

"Why are you sad?" the king asked.

"Because I have no wife," the prince sighed.

So, the next day, the king went to Lebou's father. "My son isn't old enough to be a husband and your daughter is too young to be a wife," he said. "But if you let her come to live amongst my own daughters until the pair are old enough to marry, I'll pay a fine bride price for this maiden."

So Lebou came to live amongst the other women in the king's household. A fine hut was built for her and she was given the best of everything. The king's daughters were friendly and she soon settled down. She did think it strange that no one ever mentioned the young prince whose bride she was going to be. But somehow she didn't like to ask about him. And more than a year went past quickly.

One day, after the rains, the women went out to work in the fields. After a time the king said they hadn't brought enough seed to finish planting.

"I'll run back and fetch some more," said Lebou. Off she sped back to the village. The sun was hot and when she reached the thorn hedge that ran around the compound she stopped to rest.

All at once she heard a voice shouting, "My father has got a wife for me! My father has got a wife for me!"

Lebou felt sure no man would kick up such a shocking hullaballoo inside the king's compound unless he belonged to the royal family. "It must be the one I've never seen," she gasped. "My husband-to-be." Suddenly she was desperate to see this mysterious prince. "Let him be tall," she whispered. "Let him be clever, handsome and kind."

Her intended was behaving very strangely on the other side of the hedge. "My father has got a wife for me!" the voice chortled. "My father has got a wife for me!"

The princess opened the gate in the hedge and peered around eagerly. And what should she see but a gigantic egg rolling around among the huts, shouting and laughing at the top of its voice.

"Ugh! How dreadful!" she said. "Not that round white thing." Much as she hated to touch it, she forced herself to pick up the monstrous egg. Not knowing what to do, she hid it in her hut, then went back to the fields without telling a soul what had happened.

After supper, Lebou said she wanted to sleep alone in her hut. "I've got such a headache," she said.

The moon climbed high above the trees. When the princess was sure everyone else was asleep she stole out of her hut and fled from the village. Lebou ran through the warm starry darkness on legs as strong as any warrior. Before dawn she burst into her father's hut.

"Father," she said, "why do you hate me? Why did you get rid of me so cruelly?"

"I don't hate you," said her father. "I love you dearly. And I didn't get rid of you; I arranged a wonderful marriage for you."

"A wonderful marriage!" wept the girl. "My husband isn't even a man! He's just a horrible old egg! If you loved me, you'd keep me with you and send back the bride price."

Her father didn't fancy telling such a noble king that his troublesome daughter had run away. He patted Lebou's shoulder.

"It will all work out for the best, you'll see," he said. "I know a very strong charm. Go back, do what I say and you'll have a handsome husband in next to no time."

"You'd better be telling the truth," said Lebou firmly. "Because if not I'll come straight home again."

Her father taught her the words of the charm. Then he gave her a bag of herbs and a pot of ointment and told the princess what to do.

By the time she reached her father-in-law's village everyone had gone off to the fields.

No one had noticed she was missing, supposing she was asleep in her hut. Good, thought Lebou. Now she could light a fire without anyone noticing the smoke from her hut.

She set a pot of water on the fire. While the water bubbled and boiled, she plaited rushes into a soft mat. Then she took the monstrous egg, put it carefully on the mat and poured boiling water over it – *swoosh!* – how that egg steamed!

Next, Lebou rubbed the shell with her magic ointment. It smelt of oranges, sandalwood and something which made her sneeze. She patiently rubbed the shell all over. Then Lebou covered the egg with a warm blanket, went to her sleeping mat and waited to see what would happen next.

After a while she heard a voice. "I'm growing a leg," it said in an amazed tone. "Oh, it's ve-ry long!" Everything went quiet again for a time. Then the voice announced, "Another long leg is growing." After another silence the voice shouted, "An arm. And another arm. Ooh, there's my head! And an eye. And now some ears." Finally the voice sang, "I'm all here! I'm Me! All of Me!"

Then Lebou heard a new sound – *cr-ack!* – the sound of eggshell cracking, followed by the patter of pieces of shell falling to the ground.

She jumped up, afraid of what she might find. She took a deep breath and turned back the blanket. The hut fell silent.

There, where the monstrous egg had been, lay a young man, fast asleep. He was so handsome she couldn't take her eyes off him.

But something wasn't right because her egg prince wouldn't wake up. Lebou tickled his neck with a feather. But still he slept.

The princess threw a big handful of herbs into the water to make the magic extra strong. The hut filled with a wide-awake smell. Her heart beat faster. She washed the egg prince briskly from head to toe with the warm, scented water. But still he slept.

When she'd finished washing him, Lebou rubbed the prince all over with the rest of the magic ointment. Then she gathered up the pieces of shell and dropped them in a little earthenware pot. The egg prince started to toss about.

Evening came. The girl shut the sleeping prince safely inside her hut and sat outside. The stars came out one by one. The frogs and crickets began to make their night music. At last the king's daughters returned from the fields. "Is your headache better?" they asked.

"It's worse if anything," she sighed. One of the girls brought her a bowl of steaming porridge and told her to have an early night.

But that's just what the princess didn't do.

When everyone was asleep, Lebou slipped out of the village. She ran like the wind through the glittering African night, until she reached her father's hut. "What's wrong this time?" sighed her father.

"I did everything you told me," she said. "And the egg cracked, just like you said. And out hatched a handsome prince."

"You see!" said her father. "So where is he?"

"Fast asleep in my hut," said Lebou. "What could I do? I have no clothes for a prince." So her father gave her the things an African prince must have: a cloak, a shield and a fine throwing spear. Lebou took them and hurried back. "Wake up, Prince Egg!" she whispered. "Look what I've brought you."

The prince opened his eyes and stood up. Without a word, he threw the cloak around his shoulders and took his spear and shield.

"You look very fine," she told him. "All the same, Prince Egg, you can't let anyone see you yet." And she went out of her hut, closing the door behind her, and sat down to watch the sunset.

When the king's daughters returned from the fields, they asked how she was, as before. But that evening, when they brought her supper, the girl went into her hut and secretly shared it with her silent prince.

The next morning she woke him before sunrise. "Prince Egg! Hurry! Put on your cloak and go and sit in your father's seat outside the meeting hut."

Prince Egg put on his cloak, took his shield and spear and did what she said. It was cold and misty; too early for anyone to be awake. But as the herd boys came yawning out of their huts, they were startled to see a stranger in the king's chair.

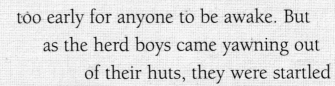

When they returned from milking the cows, the egg prince called them over. "Let me see!" he commanded. He examined the milk and told the boys to take it to the king's hut without spilling a drop.

"Master, Master! There's a stranger in your seat,"

they told the king. "He said we mustn't spill any milk! What's it got to do with him?"

The king put on his headdress and strode out to deal with this uppity stranger himself. "Who are you?" he demanded.

"Don't you know me?" said Prince Egg.

"I never saw you before in my life," said the king.

"Yet you gave me a beautiful wife," said Prince Egg, smiling.

"Did I?" asked the king, more puzzled than ever.

The prince told his father the whole story. Then he called the princess and she brought with her the fragments of eggshell she had saved.

Now the king knew the young man's story was true and that he had his longed-for son at last. Everyone was so happy that the entire village danced and sang for a week or more.

After many years the old king died and Prince Egg ruled the village in his place. Yet for some reason Lebou kept the broken eggshells. When her sisters-in-law asked her why she didn't throw them away, she only smiled mysteriously.

She didn't like to tell them the truth. For her father had told her that if ever her husband treated her badly, she only had to scatter the eggshells on his pillow and he'd go straight back into the egg from which he came.

The princess was almost certain she'd never have to do such a terrible thing. But because she was a sensible girl with her strong feet firmly on the ground, and because it's always wiser to be safe than sorry, she kept them – just in case.

WHITE-BEAR-KING VALEMON

THERE WAS ONCE A KING in Norway who had three
daughters. The two eldest were as gloomy and bad-
tempered as a pair of crows, but the youngest daughter
charmed everyone she met.

One day, the youngest daughter dreamt of a wreath of golden
flowers so wonderful she knew she'd die if she couldn't have it.
From that day on she changed. She stopped humming up and
down the castle corridors. She didn't smile. She hardly ate.
She just drifted around like a ghost.

At last the king discovered what she was pining for and commanded his goldsmith to make a golden wreath for his daughter. The goldsmith worked night and day but when the golden wreath was finished the princess scarcely glanced at it. "Thank you," she said in a dull voice. "But it's nothing like my wreath."

The next day, the princess was walking in the forest when she saw a white bear tossing something to and fro in its huge paws. It was the magical wreath of her dream. "Please let me buy it," she cried and fumbled in her purse.

"Gold cannot buy my wreath," growled the bear. "But I'll give it to you willingly if you'll be my bride tomorrow."

I don't care who I marry, so long as I have my heart's desire, thought the princess. So she eagerly agreed to his bargain and the bear gave her the wreath she longed for.

When she returned home everyone was delighted to see their favourite princess smiling again.

"Don't bother your head about that old bear," the king said soothingly. "Promises to bears don't count." However, when morning came, he posted his soldiers around the castle with their bows and arrows, to be on the safe side.

But the white bear just stormed up to the castle gate, knocking down soldiers like skittles. In desperation the king sent out his eldest daughter and at once the bear took her on his back and rushed off.

When they had travelled far, and farther than far, the bear spoke. "Have you ever sat softer, have you ever seen clearer?" he asked.

"Yes, on my mother's lap I sat softer, and in my father's court I saw clearer," squawked the princess.

"*Grrr* – then you're not the right one," growled the bear and he chased her home.

The next morning the bear swept up to the castle again.

As before, the army was under orders to deal with this annoying bear. But the bear mowed down the soldiers like grass. Finally, the king stopped the bloodshed by sending out his second daughter. The white bear took her up on his back and rushed off with her.

When they had travelled far, and farther than far, the bear asked, "Have you ever sat softer, have you ever seen clearer?"

But the second princess only squawked the same bad-tempered answer as the first.

"*Grrr*," growled the bear. "Then you're not the right one either." And he chased her home, too.

On the third day, the bear stormed up to the castle again. This time he fought so hard that the king sadly handed over his third daughter. At once the bear rushed off with her. When they had travelled far, and farther than far, he asked if she had ever sat softer and seen clearer.

"No, never," the princess said truthfully.

"Well, *you're* the right one," he said. "So you shall be my bride." When she heard his words the princess felt strangely happy, as if it were not really the wreath she had longed for, but this wild and wonderful adventure.

At last they came to a beautiful castle. "Here you are to stay and live well," said the bear gently.

To her surprise, the princess was contented in her new life. The bear was away from the castle from sunrise until sunset so she pleased herself all day. And she was delighted to discover that when evening came her husband mysteriously changed into a man. And here was another surprise. The princess found her bear-husband to

be a wise and gentle companion. In fact, as time went by, she
came to love him dearly. But since he begged her not to light the
lamp when he came to her room, the princess never once saw
his face.

After some months the princess felt homesick and asked if
she could visit her parents. The bear agreed. "But listen to what
your father says," he warned. "Not to what your mother wants
you to do."

When the princess was back home with her parents and began to
describe her life, her mother was horrified.

"You've never *seen* him!" she cried. "Take this stump of candle
and light it while he's sleeping. He'll never know. What harm can
one little peep do?"

"All the harm in the world," sighed the king. "She should leave
well alone."

97

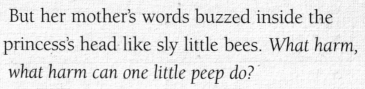

But her mother's words buzzed inside the princess's head like sly little bees. *What harm, what harm can one little peep do?*

When she was home again, she lit the candle stub and shone it on her husband's face while he slept.

Ah, but he was so handsome! She could gaze for ever and never be tired of looking. Suddenly her hand trembled. A drop of hot wax fell on his forehead and he woke.

"What have you done?" he cried. "If you had only waited one more day I would have been free. I am King Valemon. But a troll-hag enchanted me so that I must be a white bear during the day. Now I must marry her!"

"At least let me go with you," the princess pleaded. "I love you as I love my own life."

He shook his head sorrowfully. "Alas! I must leave you forever." And in front of her eyes, King Valemon became a great white bear once more.

The moment he tried to rush off, the princess seized hold of his white fur and held on for dear life. Off he went over mountains and hills, through groves and thickets, until her clothes were ripped to shreds. At last she fainted and let go.

When the king's daughter opened her eyes again she was alone in a great forest. There was nothing to do but pick herself up and carry on. As she walked along she met an old woman cutting wild herbs with some golden scissors. "Have you seen White-Bear-King Valemon?" the princess asked.

"'He rushed by earlier. But he went so fast you'll never catch up with him," the old woman replied. Then seeing that the princess's dress had been torn to ribbons, the old woman gave her the golden scissors and said, "Take these and you'll never want for clothes again."

The king's daughter thanked her and set off once more, walking day and night, until she met an old woman rinsing a golden flask in a stream.

"Good day," said the king's daughter. "Have you seen White-Bear-King Valemon?"

"Yes, he rushed by here yesterday. But he went so fast you'll never catch up with him," said the old woman. Then seeing that the princess looked thirsty, the old woman gave her the flask and said, "Take this and you'll never be thirsty again."

The king's daughter thanked her and went on her way. She walked all day and all night. On the third morning she met an old woman shaking out a golden cloth.

"Good day," said the king's daughter. "Have you seen White-Bear-King Valemon?"

"He rushed past yesterday evening. But he went so fast you'll never catch up with him," said the old woman. Then, seeing that the princess was faint with hunger, the old woman gave her the cloth and said, "Take this and you'll never be hungry again."

The princess thanked her and went on her way, walking all day and night. By sunrise she came to the side of a mountain.

It was so smooth that it seemed to go on for ever. In the shadow of the mountain a fourth old woman stood at her cottage door.

"Good morning," said the princess. "Has White-Bear-King Valemon passed this way?"

"He rushed up the mountainside three days ago," replied the old woman. "You'll never find him now. Even eagles can't get up there. Come and rest a while."

The cottage was full of ragged children crying with hunger. But the only thing on the fire was a pot full of pebbles.

"I have no food," explained the old woman. "But when I put the pot on the fire and say, 'Soon the apples will be done', it soothes them for a time."

"I'll do something about that," said the king's daughter. She brought out her flask and tablecloth and provided as much food and drink as everyone wanted. Then she snipped with her magic scissors until every child had warm clothes to wear.

"Now let me help you in your trouble," said the old woman. "My husband is a master ironsmith. If he makes iron claws for your hands and feet, perhaps you could climb the mountain."

The smith started fashioning the claws as soon he came home. When the princess awoke the next morning, they were ready. She thanked the couple and quickly fastened the claws to her hands and feet. All that day and the following night she crawled and crept up the marble-smooth face of the mountain. Then just when she couldn't drag herself another inch, she found herself at the top. There in a meadow was a great castle. Servants dashed about anxiously.

"What's going on?" the princess asked.

"In three days time the troll-hag is marrying King Valemon," she was told.

"Does he still turn into a bear when morning comes?" she asked.

"He does not. The spell was broken when he returned to marry her."

When she heard this, the princess seated herself outside the castle window and started snipping with her golden scissors. Soon silken garments flew through the air as thick as snowflakes.

When the troll-hag saw this sight she wanted to buy the scissors for her wedding. "My dressmakers have so much sewing to do they simply can't keep up," she said.

"Gold cannot buy my scissors," said the princess. "But let me sleep in your sweetheart's room tonight, and you can have them willingly."

The troll-hag agreed. But she gave King Valemon a sleeping potion so that he didn't hear the king's daughter enter his room, nor did he hear her weep and call his name the whole night long.

The next day, the princess sat outside the castle again.

This time she began pouring wine from her golden flask. But no matter how much she poured, it never ran dry. When the troll-hag saw this she wanted the flask for her wedding too.

"Gold cannot buy my flask," said the princess. "But if I may spend another night in your sweetheart's room, it's yours willingly."

The troll-hag agreed. But that night, too, she slipped a sleeping potion in King Valemon's wine. And though the king's daughter wept and called his name until morning, he didn't hear a sound.

The next day, as she sat outside the castle, the king's daughter pulled out the golden cloth, commanding it to provide delicious food of every kind. And of course the troll-hag wanted this cloth for her wedding, too.

"Then let me sleep in your sweetheart's room once more," said the princess.

Now that day, King Valemon noticed several maids yawning behind their hands. "Beg pardon your majesty," said one. "It's that girl who weeps and wails each night in your room. No-one gets a wink of sleep."

When he heard this, the king guessed what was going on. When his troll-bride brought the potion that night he took care not to drink it. And this time when the king's daughter came in and began to call his name, he answered and they embraced joyfully. King Valemon and his princess were reunited at last.

But they still had to deal with the troll-hag. So the king secretly ordered carpenters to make a trap door in the bridge which the bridal procession was to cross. When the troll-bride started out across the bridge with all her bridesmaids, the trapdoor opened.

The trolls fell into the foaming river and were never seen again.

Then the king, the princess and all the wedding guests hurried to King Valemon's castle to hold the real wedding. Everyone said it was worth waiting for as there was never such a wedding since weddings began.

And King Valemon and his bride ruled their kingdom wisely and well for the rest of their days.

ABOUT THE STORIES

THE PRINCESS & THE PEA

How can you tell if a princess is really a princess? The prince in this story has no idea. So when a bedraggled girl knocks at the castle gates, claiming to be a princess, the queen decides on a very peculiar test. In other countries, a stone or knitting needle makes the sensitive girl toss and turn in her bed. In Middle Eastern and Indian versions of this story, royal skin is so delicate, it can be bruised by a falling leaf or lotus petal.

Based on Hans Christian Andersen's well-loved story, first published in Denmark in 1835, and in England in 1846.

THE FROG PRINCESS

Stories about frog brides or bridegrooms tell us to look beneath outward appearances to find true beauty. At first, Prince Ivan is ashamed of his little frog bride. But she is wise and gentle, using her magical powers to get him out of trouble. And as Prince Ivan grows to love her, he finds the courage to stand up to his father, the bullying old Tsar.

Loosely adapted from the Russian fairytale, *The Frog Tsarevna.*

KING GRIZZLEBEARD
There's something unexpectedly modern about this lively, highly-strung and terribly rude princess! She doesn't mean to behave so badly. Her witty tongue just runs away with her. Luckily, wise King Grizzlebeard glimpses her true qualities and decides to take her in hand.

Taken from *Children's and Household Tales*, collected by the brothers Jacob and Wilhelm Grimm. Translated into English by Edgar Taylor and published in 1823 in the volume *German Popular Stories*.

THE STARLIGHT PRINCESS
The Starlight Princess and the Rajah's son were born to marry each other. Unfortunately their parents have different ideas. But this calmly radiant princess is so determined, that she completes her beloved's final and most impossible task for him.

A free adaptation of a story called *How the Rajah's Son Won the Princess Laba'm*, from *Indian Fairy Tales*, translated and privately published by Maive S.H. Stokes, Calcutta 1879.

THE SLEEPING BEAUTY

Sleeping Beauty must surely be the world's most famous fairytale princess. However the traditional ending has been altered slightly. This Beauty has the opportunity to see the world at last, after that long enchanted sleep.

From French popular tradition, first published by Charles Perrault in 1697, in a collection subtitled *Stories from Mother Goose*. Translated into English by Robert Samber in 1729.

THE TWELVE DANCING PRINCESSES

There's nothing sleepy about these mischievous princesses! Their heartlessness may be shocking, but wouldn't it be wonderful if they could carry on having fun and wearing out their silken slippers for ever? In this version that's what happens.

From the brothers Grimm.

THE EGG PRINCE

Princess Lebou is not only a brave, beautiful girl who runs faster than any warrior, she also takes good care of herself. When she releases her egg prince from his strange enchantment, she naturally hopes they will live happily ever after. But in case things don't work out, she sensibly hangs on to those eggshells.

Based on a story from Zimbabwe, translated from the Bantu by Father Torrend, and published as *Specimens of Bantu Folklore*.

WHITE-BEAR-KING VALEMON

Animal bridegroom tales follow the same pattern. A king or rich merchant's favourite daughter is tricked into marrying an enchanted beast, finds him a delightful husband, then loses him through her foolish actions. Now she must set out on a courageous journey to rescue him; in this case, from a hideous troll-hag. The adventures of this Norwegian princess begin mysteriously, with her dream of a magical golden wreath.

Adapted from *White-Bear-King-Valemon*, from *Norwegian Folk Tales*, published by The Pantheon Fairytale and Folklore Library, New York. First published in 1845 by Peter Christen Asbjornsen and Jorgen Moe.